GINGER RODEGHERO

Published by Richter Publishing LLC

www.richterpublishing.com

Book Cover Design: Richter Publishing, images from Shutterstock

Editors: Haley Morton & Rebecca Nutting

ISBN: 978-1-945812-99-6 Paperback

DISCLAIMER

DEDICATION

To the survivors of human trafficking
May your souls find peace

CONTENTS

ACKNOWLEDGMENTS

Thank you to Richter Publishing for working with me to polish my thoughts, it resulted in a much improved story for you to enjoy.

INTRODUCTION

I wrote this book to raise the awareness that human trafficking (slavery) still exists in our society today and to show how easily one could possibly be caught in the trap. The work is fictional but I have personally met and assisted individuals that were trafficked and needed a helping hand to return to normal life. It is the sequel to, "I'm Not For Sale."

PROLOGUE

A crowd was beginning to gather on the sunny Cancun beach, people strained to hear what the small Hispanic woman was telling the police. Tears streaking down her flushed cheeks, Hilda repeated for the third time what had happened to the missing children Liam and Emma, the children she had been hired to care for.

"I was sitting beside them while they were building a sand castle. Liam said he was getting thirsty and that's when I noticed the man trudging toward us with a cooler strapped to his back. People were stopping him, and he was selling them bottles of water. I told the kids I'd be right back and ran to stop him. I swear, my eyes were off them for only two minutes." Hilda gasped between sobs.

"What happened next?" Captain Reyes was hoping for new information to emerge in her story.

"I already told you." Hilda shrugged. "When I turned back, the kids were just gone." She collapsed in the sand.

Squatting beside her, Reyes looked at his fellow officer. "Get her some water."

In a soft voice he explained to Hilda, "It's a common tactic; the water guy was the distraction." She was too distraught to understand.

"How can they just disappear? All these people on the beach, how did no one see it? They vanished into thin air, right in front of hundreds of people working on their tans." Hilda scanned the growing crowd, hoping there might be one person that saw them disappear.

Handing her the cold water, Reyes continued, "That's what they count on, everyone enjoying the weather, the beach, thinking of nothing but having fun and where they'll eat tonight. It's so easy to nab a child and not be seen." Pulling Hilda to her feet, Officer Reyes guided her away from the small crowd. "I'm going to need you to come to the station so we can get a sketch of this water guy. He was in on it I'm sure. Where are their parents?"

At that, Hilda broke down anew. "What am I going to tell them? I've only been taking care of their children for a few months! They might think I'm in on this." Hilda rambled, "It was such a great opportunity for me … now I'm gonna lose my job!"

"Miss." Reyes pulled his sunglasses from his face to make direct eye contact. He needed to snap her out of the overwhelming anguish. "Where. Are. Their. Parents?"

She turned and pointed to the elaborate resort rising behind them. "They're in a seminar over there. We were supposed to meet them for dinner when they finished." Hilda collapsed into his arms.

CHAPTER 1

Christine stirred, stretching her cramped limbs. Filtered sunlight streamed through a small window. Swinging her feet to the floor, a cloud of dirt burst upward, sending bits of dust particles dancing in the light. The wooden cot creaked. She rubbed her eyes, taking in the surroundings of the small concrete room. Alongside the cot stood a small rickety table and a rattan chair. Rushing to the timber door across the room, she found it was locked … from the outside. Trapped!

Her heart was pounding. How did she end up here? Rubbing her eyes, Christine tried to clear her thoughts. What was the last thing she remembered? Her mind was cloudy. Then she saw it, she'd been in the Palazzo last night, the bar she'd been working at for the past few nights. Her parents wanted her to change up her target every few days so that she wasn't easily recognized.

She chose the Palazzo because it was packed with coeds having a good time; they had no idea there was possible danger lurking. Since coming to Cancun, she'd had to change her pick-up tactics. It wasn't like the college scene at Wellesley back in Boston. There she had time to work on one girl, pull her in with her confidence and then strike. Here she had one shot each night, tomorrow there would be a whole new group of coeds. The past few evenings had been slow, so when she walked into the Palazzo, Christine was pleased to see the dance floor was wall-to-wall bodies gyrating to the beat.

Christine targeted a blonde 20-something wrapped in a slinky, rose gold sequin dress. She knew the type that her father preferred for his business: attractive, friendly, easy to talk to, and this girl was perfect! They had been bumping and grinding on the dance floor for about an hour when Christine suggested they needed a short break and guided the blonde to a corner table where they were waiting on a drink refill.

Her ploy usually followed the same pattern. Choose a target, socialize a bit, have some drinks, get the mark a little drunk, then suggest a different bar. On the street, the pick-up was easy.

But last night something went wrong. The blonde had excused herself to use the restroom and Christine was immediately approached by a rough-looking Hispanic guy, dark hair slicked back, thin lips, a scar on his chin. She cataloged his features, including the parade of skull and scorpion tattoos running up his arms. A shiver had gripped her body.

She had tried to brush him off before her mark returned but he wasn't getting the hint. Getting up to ditch him, she felt a prick to her leg. She remembered feeling a bit nauseous, then, nothing.

The hunter had become the hunted!

****

Peering through the bars that covered the window, Christine noticed a band of young children sitting cross-legged in the dirt across the compound. Each had a small bowl resting in their laps. Her stomach grumbled.

I wonder what time it is, she thought. She'd eaten last night before going to the Palazzo but had no idea how long she'd been out. Watching the children, she wondered why they were here. Where were their parents?

Then her thoughts turned to her own parents. Were they even worried about her? She had been arguing with her father since before they even arrived in Cancun this month. His whole operation in Boston depended on her luring in acceptable prospects. But then she met Sydney and Shelby, they had been different, they could've been her first real friends. Something she'd never had during the years of war in Kosovo as a child, or even in Boston. In Kosovo she had been dragged by her parents from one safe house to the next, never quite sure if she was going to wake up the next morning with the barrel of a gun shoved in her face. She still had nightmares from the experience. In Boston, things weren't much different; the work her father did consumed her. As soon as she was old enough to get into the bars, that's where she spent her nights. But not once did she get to enjoy the music or meet any nice people to dance with. She was a pawn, there with purpose, not for fun. When she wasn't picking up girls for her father, she was kept away from most people her age by their work and her father's paranoia.

But now she couldn't stop thinking about Sydney and Shelby. She couldn't get the scene in Boston out of her mind: girls chained up in rows and rows of cots in the warehouse her father maintained. For some reason that her father refused to talk about, they'd left Boston in a hurry. They had just left the twins and the other girls there. The guilt had been gnawing at her since.

Things had changed in her world; she wanted out of his game. She'd made that clear to her father over the past few weeks. There'd been heated discussions but there was no changing her father's mind. Before leaving for the Palazzo last night, she had told him she was done! Maybe they thought she'd run away.

What's gonna happen to me? she wondered. No sooner had the thought crossed her mind when she heard a rattle at the door. The door swung open. Standing in front of her was the grizzled-looking Hispanic man from last night. His black eyes leered at her. Her heart skipped a beat.

"What were you doing in my territory?" he demanded. "I'd seen you in the Palazzo the past few nights. I watched you, I know your operation." His voice grumbled like an angry bear.

Christine didn't have an answer, she felt violated knowing someone had been following her. Searching for an ounce of courage, she glared back. "Who says it's your territory?" Sweat rolled down her back. Was it from the heat or fear?

The silence was thick, she felt he was peering into her soul.

"So, what are you going to do with me?" She needed to break his hold. "My parents will be looking for me, you know." Even as she said it, she wondered if it were true.

"Yours and all the other kids' out there," he nodded toward the courtyard. "Lunch is being served if you want some." He turned to walk away.

"Hey, wait, what's your name?" Christine needed to know who her adversary was.

"Hector," he rumbled, then he was gone.

Christine crossed the compound and sat down next to the huddled group of children. Most of them kept their heads down, quietly eating whatever was in their bowls. She studied their cowering faces; there was fear in their eyes.

She caught the wandering gaze of a small boy whose blonde hair and blue eyes made him appear almost cherub-like.

"What's your name?" she whispered softly.

She could see that he was not sure if he should speak, but his need for motherly companionship overcame his fear. "Liam."

"Hello Liam, I'm Christine." Watching him stir the bowl of gruel-like substance, she pondered what to say. How to gain his trust? Start simple!

"How old are you, Liam?" His eyes begged the young girl next to him for an answer.

"He's four, I'm Emma and I'm six." Her dark almond-shaped eyes locked with Christine's.

Christine spoke softly, "Hello Emma, I'm not going to hurt you. They had me locked in that room over there." She pointed across the compound and eight small heads turned simultaneously. That eased the tension.

"So, you are one of us?" Emma asked.

"What do you mean?" Christine was puzzled.

"We're the stolen children." Tears welled in her eyes.

She paused briefly. "Yes I suppose I am," she replied as tears pooled in her own dark eyes.

CHAPTER 2

Tim Daniels studied the two people huddled in front of his desk, stress and torment written all over them. They had met in his small office that housed the non-profit organization, "Saving Childhood." Tim's military years had opened his eyes to the travesty of human trafficking. He'd seen horrendous things, children around the world abducted and sold into bondage. That's why "Saving Childhood" had become his life mission. Something had to be done about it.

Mr. and Mrs. Walker clung to one another as if they might be ripped apart any minute.

"So, tell me why you are here." He knew the answer but needed to hear their whole story.

Taking a deep breath, William began. "My wife and I were in Cancun attending a seminar. We'd taken our two children, Emma and Liam to make it sort of a family vacation. They were on the beach with our nanny when they were nabbed."

"How long ago was that?" Tim was scratching words vehemently onto the notepad in front of him.

"It's been three months now." William broke down. "I don't know what we could have done differently. We should never have gone; we were so excited to have some family time and now it's turned into this nightmare." He rambled from one thought to another.

Tim's special forces training had honed his analytical skills, he needed to take control so that he could get the information he needed.

"This is not your fault. It's never the parents' fault. There are evil people out there and your children just happened to be in the wrong place at the wrong time." He spoke softly, he had been through this before and knew he needed to ease their guilt so that they could be productive. He saw the look that passed between William and his wife. There was relief in their eyes.

"Tell me everything from the start, then I will see if I can help."

Alicia spoke for the first time, "You have to help, we're at our wits' end. The Cancun police are getting no results." She broke down in a sob, and her petite frame shook violently.

"Alicia was the one who found your organization online, she has put all of her hope in you being able to find them." William rubbed his wife's hunched shoulders.

"I understand, I'll do my best. I've been doing this for four years and have rescued hundreds of children all over the world. But I never make a promise that I will save them, I have no idea what type of organization your children have become the victims of. I can promise you I'll do my very best to track down the criminals that have kidnapped them." He brushed his strawberry blonde waves from his soft blue eyes. His endearing smile drew them in.

William and Alicia relaxed slightly against one another.

"Now let's get to the facts and then I can work out a plan."

William started from the beginning, Tim injecting questions along the way and continuing to jot down pertinent information. He wanted to know everything the police had done thus far. Alicia gave him recent pictures of their two children. Tim immediately saw the resemblance to their mom and dad. Alicia answered questions regarding her children's personalities. This would make a difference in how they were reacting and what he might expect if he found them.

It was an exhausting two hours for everyone.

"This is what I need to do first," Tim explained. "I'll leave as soon as I can get a plane ticket and do an initial reconnaissance of the area. I need to find the kingpin in the human trafficking racket in Cancun. Generally, these types of party areas have more incidence of sex trafficking with young ladies being kidnapped and used for prostitution. This is a different scenario. These are young children. Normally, they're kidnapped and sold for other purposes."

"Do you think they may have been sold already?" Alicia experienced a new panic. "How would we ever find them?"

William and Alicia didn't want to hear the grave details but needed to face the reality of what their children are were experiencing.

"Look, let's not jump to conclusions. I need to get there and see the lay of the land, find out who could be behind this. Assess their operation and then plan. There are basic strategic ops that need to be followed to develop a sound plan."

Tim rose his 6-foot-2-inch frame from behind the desk and walked around to the two people who were putting the lives of their children in his hands. That thought always solidified his resolve to save the children.

Handing them his card, he gave them a reassuring look. "You can text me at this number and I will do my best to keep you updated. I hope to be on a plane by tomorrow night at the latest."

"Thank you, thank you." Alicia reached up and gave him a warm hug.

"Talk to you soon." He led them to the door to see them out. Returning to his desk, he sank into his chair and buried his head in his hands. Pictures of all the lost children he'd saved and the condition he'd found them in passed before his mind's eye. I hope this isn't how I find Liam and Emma, he thought. He knew from experience that it was a pipe dream.

CHAPTER 3

After two days Jetmir and Debora Kovac decided to search for Christine. They had discussed the possibility that she'd run away but Debora was sure her daughter wouldn't just take off. Jetmir wasn't so sure. His mind had replayed their last argument over and over. She had changed. She had spoken with strong conviction. Christine had made it clear she wanted out of his game.

They knew Christine had been staking out the Palazzo, so that was their first stop. Stepping into the nightclub, Jetmir was flooded with memories of the operation he'd run in Kosovo. This kind of setup was always an easy stakeout as the partiers were only concerned with having fun.

The night was young; the fun had yet to begin. Jetmir's eyes assessed the few people hanging out behind the bar and he made his decision. He pulled Debora along and made for the most likely source of information. He considered himself a good judge of character, and his target was the type of character that had secrets.

Plopping into the empty barstools, he got the attention of his mark and ordered a drink for himself and Debora.

When the drinks were settled in front of them, he broke the ice. "Hey, I have a question about a girl who might've been in here."

"Yeah, there are a lot of girls in here, that's the business." The guy made it clear he didn't want to be bothered.

Jetmir knew the tactics. Pulling a picture from his pocket, he smacked it down on the bar. "This girl, two nights ago, did you see her?"

The bartender locked eyes with Jetmir, they were the same breed: rough, aggressive, demanding. He didn't want to get into anything with this guy. He didn't have the time. A full minute ticked by as they sized each other up. Finally, the barkeep picked up the picture and studied it briefly.

"Yeah, I might have seen her, but I don't keep tabs on all the kids that are in and out of here." His gravelly voice faltered.

Jetmir recognized the attempted coverup, he'd seen it many times in Kosovo when one of his juniors didn't want to give him the full story of a flubbed operation.

"Was she with anyone? Do you know if she left with anyone? Was anyone stalking her?" Jetmir was experienced at throwing a bunch of questions at a target. The onslaught would cause confusion. Confusion equals mistakes, he listened for a slipup.

But this guy was a worthy advisory. Taking a breath, he locked eyes with Jetmir again. "I'm too busy at night to follow the affairs of every kid that comes in here. Can't help you." He turned his back and continued with the evening preparations.

Jetmir got the hint, threw a 10 on the bar, grabbed the picture and his wife's arm. At the door, he glanced back and noted that the barkeep was already on his cell.

Stepping out into the street, Debora spoke for the first time, "What did you decide? You think he knows something about her?" Her voice was on the verge of hysteria.

"Come on, I've got an idea." Jetmir wasn't going to give up so easily with this guy. He knew how to put the pressure on someone to get them to talk. This was his daughter; he'd get answers.

CHAPTER 4

Tim stepped off the plane in the hot Cancun sun. Loosening his collar and putting on his shades, he felt sweat already rolling down his back.

He'd spent the past two days searching the dark web, hunting for his target. He'd made a list of potential organizations, but his first stop was the police station. He had to make himself known and find out what information they had gathered since Liam and Emma's disappearance.

As the taxi jockeyed through the streets, he took a moment to reflect on his own three children. Looking at the picture of Liam and Emma, he tried to imagine how he'd feel if it were his kids he was searching for. He felt William and Alicia's pain. There was a certain mental anguish he experienced every time he took on a new case. He'd failed on a few missions and didn't want to add Liam and Emma to that list.

Tim's eyes had been opened when he had worked the US Border Patrol. Children were bought and sold. Yes, he had managed to save many who were being smuggled across the border, but he also knew there were thousands of children that had been trafficked and no one was there to rescue them. He didn't want to know what they were enduring but he had rescued enough victims that the truth was heart-wrenching.

Stepping into the Cancun Police Station he headed for the officer behind the plexiglass window.

"Sir, I'm Tim Daniels. I have an appointment with Captain Reyes."

The officer checked the notes in front of him. "Yes, I have your name here. Please have a seat. Captain Reyes will be with you shortly."

Tim sat quietly watching the hustle of the busy station. He was no stranger to the inner workings of a police station, so he rapidly assessed the level of expertise around him. Watching two officers manhandle a rowdy, drunken college student, he figured that was the daily norm.

"Mr. Daniels?" His attention was drawn to a tall officer who looked more like a teddy bear than someone who faced hardened criminals.

"Captain Reyes, it is a pleasure to meet you." Tim reached out his hand and was met with a firm grasp. He made note that Officer Reyes was obviously tougher than he appeared.

"Please join me in my office." They headed down a dingy hall, bare light bulbs hanging overhead. Crossing the threshold to his office, Captain Reyes spoke in Spanish to the lady sitting at the desk outside his door, sending her to get them water.

"Please sit down." Reyes directed Tim to a rough wooden chair across from his small cluttered desk. "Not like America, I know, but we make do." The door opened and two water bottles were deposited on the desk. The petite, dark-haired woman quickly exited. "I understand you're down here regarding the Walker children. I appreciate that you came to visit here before embarking on your investigation." Captain Reyes' soft, low voice had Tim thinking teddy bear again.

"There is no reason for me to dig around in areas you've already covered. I'd like to know everything that you have uncovered and then I can move forward." Tim knew better than to step on the toes of local police; he needed them to be his ally.

"We have a very interesting mix of ... hmmmm, let's call them entrepreneurs. We of course have those who are working to entertain and care for all of the tourists that come to Cancun." He shrugged. "Then we have those who support themselves by taking advantage of those same tourists. Captain Reyes opened his water and took a long swig.

"You know the history of Cancun?" Reyes arched his brow, waiting for Tim to take the bait.

"I believe it was developed using a computer model." Being that history was his college major, Tim knew a bit about Mexico.

"In 1970 this booming resort town was just a poor fishing village with about 120 residents, give or take a few," Reyes began. "The Mexican government decided that tourism meant money. They turned over the job of creating a resort town to a 40-year-old Harvard-educated entrepreneur. Taking every measurable parameter into account, he fed all the data into a computer. They were looking for a potential site that had perfect weather year-round, blue skies and bluer seas. White sand beaches lined with towering palms. There had to be drinking water available, few mosquitos, fewer snakes and minimal off-shore sharks. A lot of time and consideration was put into selecting a location. Cancun met all criteria, so this beautiful oasis was created out of the fishing village. For Mexico, it meant tourism money, resorts, restaurants, shopping, beaches. For me it means ... well you're here ... for me it's daily headaches." Tim noticed Reyes' soft brown eyes had hardened. "I wish you were here to see my beautiful country, not to tour its underbelly." Captain Reyes stretched back in his chair; Tim saw the change occur. The teddy bear vanished, and a vicious predator took its place. "Would they have created this party town if they'd known the evil that would follow?" Tim wondered if the captain wanted an answer or if the question was merely rhetorical. "I go on too long, let me help you … I hope I can help you. I understand lost children are your specialty, maybe you can help us."

"I have done some preliminary research on the dark web where you can find anything for sale" Tim began, "I have located an organization down here that seems to specialize in marketing children. Their front is orphanages. I've narrowed it down to one in particular." Tim watched closely to see if Reyes reacted to the news.

The captain's brow creased. "I am so busy with drug rings and prostitution rings that this is not an area I had thought to investigate. We periodically get missing children. There is a scam the kidnappers use on the beach but to date, sadly we've had no luck in recovering any of these children. I hate to speak to the parents because I feel so helpless when I have no answers. I can't imagine if it were one of my own children."

Tim pulled out his notepad and began with the list of questions he had drawn up. He needed to know what exactly had been done and how much, if anything, Reyes knew about the child trafficking that was going on under his nose. When he asked about St. Cecil's Orphanage, Reyes jolted. He was clearly shocked. "I see you have some knowledge of this organization." Tim's instincts were alerted.

Reyes hung his head, shaking it in disbelief. "Please do not tell me this is the orphanage you suspect."

"Yes, this is where my research has led me. What do you know about them?"

"My church supports this orphanage."

CHAPTER 5

The daily routine of the orphanage was easy to follow. They were constantly monitored by the orphanage director. The children's welfare seemed to be of little concern. Their clothes were dirty, their hair unkept, and the food was sparse and tasteless.

Christine had been there less than a week, but little had changed. She spent time with the children during the day and was locked back up each night. She rapidly became the surrogate mother of the small band, with Liam attached to her like a tick to a dog.

Gaining the children's trust, she had managed to pull from each of them their name, where they came from, how they happened to be here. Most had been plucked off the sandy beach in broad daylight. Christine had little prior involvement with children, but they were rapidly becoming, for her, the only beauty in this dismal place.

She knew the children were missing their families. She'd held each of them as they told their story, tears filling their eyes. Christine realized she had something in common with them, besides being stuck where they didn't want to be, she'd experienced the same fear as a child. Growing up in Kosovo during a war was an endless nightmare, the constant uncertainty of her future, the threat of being caught or even killed. Her childhood reality was being lived by these children.

Still, there were moments when the small band of ragamuffins would let go of their fear and have good, old fun, chasing chickens, playing tag, creating games out of rocks and sticks. How did they manage to be so resilient?

Christine hadn't seen Hector since he'd let her out of the cell. She had no idea what her future held. However, today was different. When she was released from her cell, she sensed something was in the air. The director was bustling around the anxious kids, wiping their faces, changing them into clean clothes which had appeared from nowhere, putting shoes on their dusty feet. She listened intently as they were given specific instructions.

"You're all to be on your best behavior," the director stated sternly, "there will be a lady and gentleman here who would like to adopt a child and take them home."

Christine heard nothing after that remark, as an alarm went off in her head. She knew each child's story, none of them should be adopted. She saw the panic on their small innocent faces when the announcement was made. Liam ran to Christine and hid behind her petite frame.

"No one can take me," he whispered. "How will mommy and daddy find me if I leave here?" His small body shook.

She picked him up and held him close. "I'll get you out of here and back to your parents somehow," she assured him.

He laid his small blonde head on her shoulder. "Promise?"

"Promise!" she vowed. Deep down, Christine didn't know how she could ever keep that promise. A picture of her own parents flashed in her mind's eye. Would she ever see them again?

CHAPTER 6

Jetmir had put his own prostitution business on hold, spending his days stalking the bartender. He knew his pattern. Sleep most of the day, get to the bar around four in the afternoon, head home after chasing the last partier out well after three in the morning. The bartender usually staggered home so he was an easy mark.

It was only mid-morning, but Jetmir had nodded off due to his late-night surveillance. He was jolted awake by the vibration in his pocket. Digging out his phone, he saw it was Debora.

"Yeah?" He was a bit groggy from the days of tracking his adversary.

"Do you know anything?" Debora's voice was strained.

"You know these things take time. To defeat the enemy, you must understand their every move." As he spoke, the bartender emerged from his apartment, breaking his pattern of the past few days.

"Listen, he's on the move; something's up. I'll call you when I have news." Tossing his phone on the passenger seat, he started the car, ready for whatever was next.

The bartender stood on the curb lighting a cigarette. After a few puffs, a black limo pulled up and he jumped in. Jetmir watched as they pulled slowly away, then eased out a few cars behind, not wanting to draw attention.

The driver looked familiar, Jetmir thought he'd seen him at the Palazzo when they'd first been there. Maybe this was the man to follow, maybe he'd lead them to Christine.

They drove away from the resort area, out into a rural district. After about 30 minutes Jetmir watched as the limo pulled up to the entrance of St. Cecil's Orphanage. The wide gate was rolled aside and the limo crept through. Jetmir inched his car by the opening, straining to see inside. He spotted a small band of children huddled in the center of the compound. There was a young lady holding a small blonde boy. From the back, her frame looked similar to his daughter's, but what was she doing here … at an orphanage? Had she run away to here? Why an orphanage? The gate was rolled shut before he could confirm if it really was Christine.

Could it really be her? None of this made sense.

Picking up his phone he dialed Debora. "I may have something." He explained to his wife where he was and that he may have seen Christine.

"Maybe it's just wishful thinking," Debora didn't want to build false hopes.

"Maybe … but something is strange here, I'm going to hang out a bit to see what develops. When tracking a foe, you have to take any lead he gives you. Talk to you soon." He ended the call and stared at the big wooden doors, wishing he could see through them.

CHAPTER 7

Tim met Captain Reyes at 10 in the morning. Stepping into the captain's office, he was stunned by the beauty of the lady speaking with Reyes.

"Tim, this is Officer Garcia." Captain Reyes was in his teddy bear mode. "She's been completely briefed on your proposal."

"It's nice to meet you." Extending his hand, Tim was met with a slim, delicate grasp. "You will be perfect for this charade." He wanted to be sure that the lady who posed as his wife met certain criteria for the scene they needed to portray.

"It is an honor to work with you. Captain Reyes has told me of your organization and of the children you have rescued. I must say, I was stunned to hear that this orphanage may be trafficking children right under our noses. If that is so, I really want to be part of taking

31

them down." The passion in her voice confirmed for Tim that she was perfect for the job.

"I've made arrangements with the director for us to visit with the children and see if there are any who may meet our requirements. The backstory I have given them is that we cannot have children and we would like to adopt siblings if possible. I don't want you to be surprised if the story changes when we get there. If things go as I suspect, these children are not orphans and are being sold for a very different purpose. So please play along." Tim had been through this before so he knew things could go sideways very rapidly.

"I'll follow your lead. Any other orders?" Officer Garcia was all business.

"Just one thing, your first name?"

"Maria."

"Alright Maria, let's do this." He pulled the picture of Emma and Liam from his pocket. Maria had seen it before. "I'm hoping to spot these children, they are my primary mission but if this orphanage is marketing children …" He stopped, his heart was pounding, a cold chill grasped his soul. This was the emotion that always surfaced when he went into action.

"I understand." Marla's tone was on edge.

"Your car is ready." Captain Reyes directed them to police parking in the rear of the building. "Maria knows the way."

"Thank you, Captain, let's hope we're on the right track." Tim took the keys and opened the passenger door for Officer Garcia. "Shall we, Maria?" She climbed into the car and he pushed it closed.

"Good luck." Captain Reyes saluted.

Tim returned the gesture and got in behind the wheel. He was in full alert mode. This was a reconnaissance mission. He hoped to give the Walkers a favorable report.

CHAPTER 8

Jetmir was still parked outside St. Cecil's when Tim pulled up to the gate. As the white Pontiac crept through the opening, he saw the bartender and his driver posed to greet the arriving party. The children weren't visible. He jotted the name of the orphanage on an old napkin he'd found stuffed in the adjacent seat. Then he started his car and turned back toward town. He had an idea to get inside those walls, and he was headed to put the plan in motion with his wife.

* * * * * * * * * * * * * * * * * * * *

Tim pulled the vehicle to a stop, hopped out and raced around to open the door for Maria.

"Thank you for meeting with us on such short notice, Mr. Soto." Tim extended his hand in a casual manner, but he was observing and mentally recording everything about the people he was meeting and the surrounding compound. He noted the line of skull and spider tattoos running up Soto's forearm, which seemed odd for someone running an orphanage.

"Please, call me Hector. This is my assistant, Raoul. It's no problem to meet with you. The children always love to have visitors."

"Where are they?" Maria appeared very anxious. *She's a good actress*, Tim thought.

"They're still getting ready for your visit. If you could come with me, I'd like to get an idea of what you and your husband want the children for." Hector extended his arm across Maria's shoulder. Tim made note of the visible shudder that ran through her body. Something about his words or touch had just creeped her out.

Tim knew it was time to change his ploy, he had this guy marked now for exactly what he was. He wasted no time in changing his story to keep Hector on the string.

"We are looking for very specific children, who can be used to bring pleasure." Tim had used this routine before but it always hurt his heart to think that any adult would have ugly intentions for a child's future.

Hector took the bait and went down the line Tim was searching for. "We have lots of adults coming here to … uh … should I say, purchase children for their business. Raoul, bring the children to the compound so Tim and his wife may look at them." His emphasis on "wife" made it clear to Tim that Hector knew they weren't married.

The band of children were led into the compound, their innocent faces screaming fear. There was a young woman among the group. Tim thought this odd, and he wondered how she played into the story.

Hanging on her leg was a small blonde boy. Tim recognized him immediately: Liam. A quick scan and he spotted Emma in the middle of the huddle. His heart skipped a beat, but he needed to stay on point and not expose his true mission. Emma and Liam were his main target; however, the other children were probably kidnapped too. He wanted to take down the whole operation if he could.

Tim and Maria strolled casually around the group of children acting as if they were assessing the marketability of the children. Tim was actually making note of the health of each child and Maria was matching faces to pictures of other children who had gone missing.

Tim squatted down to Liam's level and peered into his innocent cherub face.

"Looks like you might be good at sports," Tim's friendly tone was met with a small upturned smile. Emma wasn't as trusting and immediately moved to her brother's side, wrapping her arm around his tiny shoulder.

"You can't take him," Emma barked. Tim immediately saw the resemblance to her mother. She wore the same strained expression Alicia had at their meeting. *These kids are experiencing a stress I can't imagine*, he thought.

The tall slender lady moved quickly to shelter them both, giving Tim a fierce grimace raising an alarm in his mind. *What does she have to do with this*? he wondered.

Standing to his full height, Tim gave Maria a slight nod.

She took the cue. "Where can we talk further?"

"Christine, the children are dismissed," Hector barked.

Now I have a name for her, Tim thought, making a mental note to search for her likeness among the missing person's photos at the police station.

"This way." Hector directed them toward what appeared to be a small office. Stepping inside, Tim took inventory of all access points. Not knowing how this was going to play out, he needed to plan for all options.

Hector wasted no time getting down to business, turning to Maria. "Do you have your heart set on any child in particular?" He gave her a twisted sneer. "Each child you purchase is $50,000 paid in cash. We meet at a prearranged location. After I collect the money, the children will be turned over to you."

There was clearly no negotiating. Tim played along. "We are interested in the siblings. Give us a day or two to arrange the cash transfer and we'll be in touch."

"Can we visit the children again?" Maria questioned. Tim could see that she was working out a plan in her mind too.

"The children are tired now." Hector's tone made it clear the visit was over.

"We'll be in touch," Tim directed Maria out the door and toward the car. They pulled slowly from the courtyard out onto the dirt road, without speaking a word. Once Tim could see in his rearview mirror that the entrance was well behind them, he finally spoke.

"It's a good thing we wore these wires." He retrieved the small bug from under his collar. "Now all we have to do is exchange the money and we'll have all we need to indict Hector and his buddy on human trafficking."

"I hope it works out that easily." Maria sounded as if she had her doubts.

"Sometimes it does, sometimes it doesn't." Tim knew from experience not to plan on the simple route.

"Anyway, let's get back to the station and work out the next step with Captain Reyes." Maria laid her head back and closed her eyes. A single tear rolled down her check.

****

Hector leaned back in his chair, feet propped on his desk, a cigarette dangling in his hand. Raoul was sitting across from him in a straight-back wooden chair. No words had yet to be exchanged, both were mentally spending their future earnings.

There was a timid knock and the director poked her head in the door. "We have a call from another gentleman who is interested in seeing the children. He'd like to come out with his wife later today."

"Well, well, this could be our lucky day." Hector laughed out loud. "Guess we'll have some lunch here. What're the names of the couple coming?"

"Jetmir and Debora," she replied. Then she left to get the children's lunch ready.

"Well, well, profits rolling in." Hector took a drag from his cigarette and blew smoke rings into the air.

CHAPTER 9

Maria and Tim settled in Captain Reyes' office, drinks were brought in and they both took a moment to organize their thoughts.

"We have everything recorded, somehow this organized ring has been operating right under our noses. I'm sorry to say I didn't expect this." Reyes held his head in shame.

"My heart broke for those poor children. I felt their fear when I looked in their eyes." Maria wiped a tear from her cheek.

"This is an area I'm very familiar with. Worldwide children are typically trafficked for the uses of illegal adoptions, child soldiers, sex slavery or to work for an organized crime group. The US

State Department officials estimate that roughly 1 million children work as domestic servants in Latin America alone. I try to function very analytically when approaching these missions, but when I see the actual victims my heart breaks. It only serves to solidify my mission." Tim spoke with a deep-seated passion.

"We're with you until the end on this one, my eyes have been opened." Reyes wasn't in a teddy bear frame of mind. The tiger in him growled.

"We need to organize the money drop. We'll need cameras and microphones so we can record every bit of the exchange." Tim had set up these sting operations before and was creating a mental battle plan. "I can get that kind of money together from some of my non-profit donors. They are familiar with these set-ups and know they'll get the funds back."

"What's the next move with Hector?" Maria was tracking with Tim's plan.

"We'll contact him in the morning and inform him we have the cash together, set up the meet point so we can get all the surveillance in place ahead of time and coordinate the time for the exchange."

"Do these things ever fall apart?" Maria wanted to know what to be prepared for.

"You can never predict exactly how it will play out but remember, I have managed to rescue hundreds of children. Every child saved means another trafficker is brought down."

"Alright, we meet in the morning." Reyes was set. "Tim, I really appreciate your help in this mission. With the intel you've gathered, we'll make many parents happy when we end this nightmare."

Tim stood up, "I need to call my donors. I'll be here first thing in the morning to set this plan in motion." As he walked out of the office, he heard Reyes in full SWAT mode ordering his team to get together the necessary equipment.

CHAPTER 10

Christine was sitting in the courtyard surrounded by the band of children. Liam was cuddled up in her lap. They'd just finished their lunch and she was entertaining them with a folktale her mother had told her long ago.

Suddenly, she stopped mid-sentence as another car was admitted into the compound. The laughing ceased as all the children turned to see what had interrupted the fun. Christine's heart surged when she saw her own parents step from the car. She watched Hector approach them. How had they found her? Were they here to get her out? What about Liam and the others? Her mind raced.

Hector walked up to Jetmir and Debora, playing the same routine he had earlier with Tim and Maria.

"So, what type of child will serve your purpose?"

Jetmir was scanning the compound and saw the children huddled around Christine. They locked eyes.

"I'm not really interested in a child. I have my eye on that young lady over there," Jetmir responded. "She would be perfect."

"Boss, can we talk?" Raoul interjected.

Hector lashed back, "You're not to get involved in these discussions."

Raoul shrunk back but continued, "Sorry, but I know something you need to know ..." He stuttered, "It'll, uh, it's important."

"Better be." Hector turned to Jetmir. "Please excuse the interruption."

Raoul took a few steps from Jetmir and his wife. "Sorry ..." He hesitated again. "That's the guy ..." he whispered.

"What guy? What are you talking about?" Hector's face scowled.

"The guy that came to the bar … asking about her!" Raoul turned and pointed to Christine. "He's the one that had her picture."

"Well, well," mumbled Hector. "That changes the negotiations." Hector headed across the compound toward the children. When he approached Christine, he saw the shock on her face. "How did he find you?"

Christine's mouth was dry, and the children were cowering behind her. "I have no idea," she checked herself and tried to put on a brave front. "I believe you've met your worst nightmare."

Hector broke out into an uproarious laugh. "We'll see about that." He grabbed her by the arm and dragged her across the compound. Debora couldn't contain herself, she raced to wrap her arms around Christine as if she were still a small child in the bunkers of Kosovo.

Jetmir didn't hesitate. "I'll be leaving with my daughter now." He attempted to guide Christine and Debora toward the car, but Hector stepped into his path.

"You send your daughter into my territory where she works my marks, and then somehow you think I should just return her to you as if no line has been crossed!" Spittle sprayed from his mouth as his anger intensified.

Christine had never seen her father back down from any advisory, but she didn't miss that he winced when Hector got in his face.

"I have the upper hand here and I will tell you what happens with your daughter." Hector turned and pointed across the compound. "You see those children? I get $50,000 a head. Now your daughter is not the age my clients are normally looking for, so I will give her back to you at a reduced price … let's say $35,000 for all my trouble, and you get out of town and don't interrupt my business again." His steely eyes locked on Jetmir.

There was a long silence as they studied each other. Jetmir knew he'd met his match. This wasn't his domain, he just wanted to get Christine out of bondage. Finally, he nodded. "Alright, I'll get you the money."

Christine had been watching the exchange. "I won't leave without Liam and Emma," she blurted out. Everyone was stunned but not as surprised as Christine. She didn't know where the courage had come from, but she wasn't leaving them here to be sold.

Hector threw back his head and belted out an uncontrolled laugh.

"We can't do that," Debora spoke for the first time. "I mean what would we do with them?"

Gathering her fortitude, she continued, "I promised them, I'm going to get them home!"

All eyes were on her; she stood her ground.

"Well, she is a feisty one." Hector was still laughing, "Maybe I've underestimated her value."

"Christine …" Jetmir's eyes blazed. This wasn't the time or place for them to continue the argument they'd had before she disappeared.

"I'm not leaving without them!"

"Yeah … feisty. Well, I do have another couple who are interested in them." Hector's mind was racing, how could he get the most out of this? "Tell you what, you pay me the $50,000 per child and I'll throw in Christine here for another $25,000. That's a bargain."

Christine felt like a piece of meat, how could one bargain for another human life?

"I'll get it. We'll be in touch." Jetmir turned and grabbed Debora's arm, leading her toward their car.

"Don't take long, I expect my other buyers to be in touch tomorrow." Hector was pleased with himself, knowing he had the upper hand.

Christine watched as her parents pulled out of the compound. *How are they ever going to come up with that money?* she wondered. But knowing her father, she figured he had a plan. As she headed back toward the children, she was met halfway by Liam. He wrapped his tiny arms around her slender legs. There was a new fear in his face. Gradually prying him from her, she picked him up and held him tight. His small body was shaking.

"It's OK, Liam," she whispered, "I'm going to take care of you." Somehow, she was going to keep that promise.

CHAPTER 11

Tim had worked late to organize the money but still arrived early the next morning to Captain Reyes' office. They were huddled together, discussing how to handle the upcoming call. Everyone sat in silence as he picked up his phone to set up the meet. He noticed Maria's nervous twitch as the phone rang. He gave her a gentle smile, mouthing, "It will be OK."

His heart stopped when Hector picked up. "You got the money?"

"You assumed it was me?" Tim fired back.

"Well, let's just say, we're on the same wavelength."

"Where do we meet?" Tim wanted to regain control.

"I have a room reserved for you at the Sun Palace, show them your ID and they will give you the key." Captain Reyes was making notes as Hector spoke. "Bring the money and we will make the drop arrangements from there. Let's say 2 pm." The phone disconnected before Tim could say another word.

There was not a sound in the room, as Tim was calculating his next move.

"I'll get my crew down there immediately to get all the wiretaps and cameras in place. I've had an undercover guy on Hector since your meeting yesterday. Apparently, he owns the Palazzo. We've had some incidents occur there but never anything that would shut him down. We'll keep a watch on him and let you know when he is headed toward the Sun Palace."

Tim nodded but his mind was playing all of the possible scenarios and his trained responses. The military had drilled him well and he needed all of his skills to rescue Liam and Emma.

"OK Maria, we've got some work to do. Let's go." Tim wanted to take the time to walk through the next move with her.

CHAPTER 12

Jetmir studied the view provided by the drone that soared across the landscape toward the orphanage. The jungle-like foliage, the view of the water rolling gently onto the beach, tropical birds flying alongside the drone ... he felt a moment of peace.

"There's the orphanage compound," Debora interrupted his solitude. "Look for Christine." The flutter in her voice gave away her fear.

"Look, I know you're worried but what I'm trying to do is find a way that I can sneak into the compound and rescue our daughter. We know she's there, and we need to figure out a way to get her out."

He quietly directed the drone around the perimeter of the wooden walls, checking all entrances, where the walls could be easily scaled, where there would be good ground coverage. His years as a lieutenant in the Kosovo Liberation Army had taught him all he needed to survive any attack by sneaking up on the opponent, catching them off guard. He had to get an idea of where they may be holding Christine at night, so he guided the drone over the open courtyard. To the left of the entrance they had driven through was a small office. Beside that was what might be another office, but there was an open padlock hanging loosely from a latch. He made note. Across the dirt compound was where the children must sleep as it appeared to be some kind of dorm space. Overall, the facility was old, the boards weathered and warped, not a difficult fortress to breach.

"I wish I'd had one of these in Kosovo," he commented. Even though the drone was silent, it had caught the children's attention and soon they were playfully chasing after it. He saw Christine studying the drone. He watched as she swooped up a small blonde boy and swung him in a playful circle. He hoped she realized her father was coming for her.

Handing the control fob to his wife, he grabbed a paper and sketched out the layout of the compound. He had an idea of how to get in and out quickly.

Putting down the drawing he inhaled deeply. "We need to call this Hector guy and make him think we're getting the money together. That way they won't be expecting our hit."

He guided the drone to a landing where he could grab it later. Then, picking up his phone, he watched his wife's nervous agitation, wringing her hands and wiping her brow. He had seen these cues many times in their married life.

"It's going to be OK. We'll walk through the plan as soon as I finish here."

"Hello?" Hector didn't seem to be expecting his call.

"We have the money, I'll come tomorrow with the funds and I'll be taking my daughter with me." He wanted to take control of the situation rapidly.

"Well OK, does that include funds for the two kids?"

Jetmir paused, might as well play the game. "Yes."

"Now this changes things." Hector's deep chuckle left no room for a response.

"Tomorrow, let's say 2 pm, I'll come to the orphanage. See you then." Jetmir rapidly disconnected the phone; he had to show control.

"This is the plan …" He reviewed with his wife exactly what he envisioned. When he was through, he looked into her pleading eyes. "It will work," he added reassuringly. "We'll hit just before dawn, low light, easier to hide in the shadows. Now let's go through this again."

CHAPTER 13

The *tick tock* of the wall clock added to the tension in the room, and Tim paced the floor in rhythm to the beat. They'd not heard from Captain Reyes yet. What could be the delay? Three minutes past the agreed time, Tim applied his deep-seated training. Stop, look, listen, smell. Use every sense to assess the scene and mentally prepare.

Maria strolled across the room and poured a small glass of water, and the ice clanked in the cup as her hands shook. The suitcase of cash was lying on the bed.

A sharp rap on the door. Tim's heart stopped. He strolled toward the door, feeling as if he was in a time warp focusing on every move. As he turned the knob, Raoul barged into the room and slapped an envelope into Tim's hand.

"Later," he bleated out, and exited the room as rapidly as he'd come in.

Tim and Maria stood like two statues in a park, shock punctuating their faces.

Captain Reyes raced into the room from the adjoining suite where his command station had been set up. "What just happened?"

Tim ripped open the envelope and silently read the communication. "This changes everything." He handed the note to the captain who read it out loud.

"We have another buyer. The price has changed to $100,000 per child. Tomorrow before noon or they will be gone."

"Sounds like our man is getting greedy." The captain dropped the note on top of the suitcase containing the purchase funds. "What do you suggest?" He had an idea of what they needed to do but trusted Tim's experience.

"First, I can't get those funds together by noon tomorrow. Second, we can't trust that he won't change the game again. Third, looks like Liam and Emma are out of time. We need to act before they are gone." Tim rapidly calculated all options.

"Agreed, I say we hit the compound and bust up the whole operation. We have enough on these guys to put them away now. Let's go get all the children." Captain Reyes had that tiger fierce tone, there was no messing with him now.

"In the morning, just after sunrise. We want there to be some light so we can be sure all the children are secure. You never know, there could be shots fired." Tim was speaking from an all too familiar experience. He didn't want to share those horrible details.

They packed up the rooms and headed to the station to work out the new plan of attack.

CHAPTER 14

Hector was sitting in his office at the Palazzo. The phone call had piqued his curiosity.

"What's happening boss?" Raoul had just returned from his errand to the Sun Palace.

"Just got a call from the orphanage. There was a drone flying around the compound earlier. Now, who would be snooping on children?" Tapping a pencil against his chin, Hector was weighing all possibilities. Raoul knew better than to interrupt his thoughts.

"I think we should spend the night at the orphanage, just in case. Give that director lady a little break. We'll go after we close up here." He was speaking but still seemed to be in deep thought.

"Excuse me …" Raoul was trying not to agitate his boss.

Hector finally snapped from his thoughts. "Uhhh … yes! Bring the guns from here. You never know … we may need to protect the children." His grumble made it clear that was the least of his concerns.

CHAPTER 15

Christine thought she was dreaming. She heard her father calling her name, then a gentle tap on her shoulder. She rolled over and found herself staring into Jetmir's dark eyes.

"Baba." She bolted upright. "You came for me; how did you get in?" She was trying to process what she was seeing. Trying to make sure it wasn't a dream.

Jetmir kissed her softly on her forehead. "Come on, quickly … We must get out of here before the sunrise."

Christine hugged her father fiercely. "I had no idea what was going to happen to me. How did you ever find me?" All of her anger toward her father dissipated.

"Come on, come on." He gently pulled her toward the door. "I'll explain later, but we must hurry."

Christine headed toward the door of her small cell, still trying to understand what was happening. How many times as a child had they had to sneak away in the dark? How many times had her life been in jeopardy? Then she stopped short, thinking of her childhood fears, she remembered Liam.

"I can't go without Liam and Emma." She stood firm.

"We don't have time for this; we need to get out of here." Frustration was building in Jetmir's voice.

"I made them a promise, and I won't leave them to be sold like animals. I understand their fear. I need to do this." She locked eyes with her father. He saw in her a strong resolve that he had felt in himself many times. He knew there was no point in arguing, as dawn was minutes away.

"Alright, where are they …? We must hurry."

"This way, I'll lead you to their dorm." Christine bolted out the door but Jetmir grabbed her elbow.

"We need to move quietly and stay in the shadows. We can't be discovered, or this could go wrong very rapidly." His instructions were firm.

"OK." She stretched up on her toes and gave him a quick peck on his cheek. "Thank you, Baba. This way."

Leaving what had been Christine's cell, they crept along the perimeter of the courtyard. Christine led her father to the small dorm where eight tiny bodies lay still, almost lifeless. Signaling her father toward one small mound, she hustled to the next bed. Jetmir gently picked up Emma while Christine pulled the blanket off Liam.

Liam roused. "What's happening?" He rubbed his sleepy eyes "What are we doing?"

Christine put her fingers to his lips. "Shhhh, I'm taking you home now."

Liam climbed into her arms and laid his head on her shoulder. "Thank you," he whispered.

Jetmir, carrying Emma who was still in a deep sleep, led Christine to the spot he had used to break in. There was a small drainage access that he had dug out and crawled through. He sent Christine back through first, and Liam followed. Gently rousing Emma, he passed her to Christine on the other side. Emma seemed to understand that they needed to be quiet. Debora was waiting in the car and grabbed the children as they piled in. Liam crawled over and cuddled up on Christine's lap, while Emma laid her head against Debora's shoulder and closed her eyes.

"Thank you, Christine," Emma whispered. "When will I get to see my mama?"

"Soon, I promise ... soon." Christine laid her head back and pulled in a deep sigh. She was safe again, but she was not done with her mission.

Jetmir pulled slowly away from the orphanage just as the sun peeked over the horizon.

Heading toward town, he glanced in the rearview mirror and saw shadows of dark figures headed toward the front doors of the orphanage.

"We got out just in time, look." He motioned to Debora who turned in her seat and saw a squad of armed men approaching St. Cecil's.

"Go quickly, get us away from here." Debora had tears in her eyes. "Please, let's leave this city."

"Not before I get Liam and Emma back to their parents," Christine chimed in. "I know what it feels like to have your parents back!"

"How do you propose to find their parents?" There was a hint of anger in her father's voice.

"I don't know …" she stammered. "I'll find them somehow."

Emma picked her head up and answered, "I know my mommy's phone number, she made me memorize it for emergencies."

"That's great, we'll call her in the morning." Christine was happy that a solution had presented itself so easily. "First, we need to get you to safety, then we will call."

She laid her head back and ran through her mind what she would say to the children's parents. Her thoughts were interrupted by Liam.

"When can we go home?"

"Soon, Liam, soon." She hugged him tight.

CHAPTER 16

Tim and Captain Reyes team were lined up outside the entrance to the orphanage. He was making a final mental scan of their plan before he gave the signal. The sun was on the horizon, and Tim spotted a car in the distance headed toward town. An alarm went off; it seemed odd for there to be any traffic on this quiet road at this hour. Making a mental note, he turned toward the captain. Giving a thumbs up, Reyes signaled his team into action.

The doors gave way with a loud crack as the battering ram splintered it into fragments. The team crept into the compound and fanned out. Within seconds, there were pounding feet and voices yelling directions. Tim hadn't expected there to be resistance, but things don't always go as planned.

Captain Reyes directed one crew toward the coming onslaught and another group toward the dorm. The children's safety was top priority.

Tim wanted to secure Emma and Liam but that was not his assignment. He needed to trust Maria and her team to corral the kids safely. Tim was slinking through the compound ... he halted ... stop, look, listen, smell. He was hoping this was not a trained band of attackers coming at him. His senses were on full alert.

Tim and five police officers surrounded the courtyard, weapons ready. Before long he saw the shadows of four men fanning out.

Tim noticed they weren't covering each other's backs ... *Good, easier to bring them down if needed.* Just as the thought passed through his head, a shot rang out, hitting the splintered door behind them. Taking fire was something he was used to, but one never knew how it would play out, especially if the opponent was just being reactive and wasn't well-trained.

Tim directed several of Reyes' men with him, and headed in the direction of the office, planning to flank the small band. Captain Reyes distracted their attention by firing a few wide shots over their heads. Coming up behind them, there was no contest. Tim and the officers each nabbed a man, stripped them of their guns and drove them to the ground. Reyes brought his team over and handcuffed the courtyard gang.

Then another shot rang out. Tim's heart was pounding in his ears … The kids. Running toward the dorm, he hoped the children were safe.

Coming up behind Maria, she startled when he tapped her shoulder.

"I saw two men duck in there just now with the children. They fired a wild shot. I think just to scare us. What's the next move?"

Tim rapidly assessed the outside of the dorm space. He saw two windows on the south wall. "You stay here, keep their attention on the door. I'm headed around to the back side and will set up a rear ambush. Don't fire any shots if at all possible."

He slung his gun over his shoulder and began to scale the outside of the dorm using a small ledge that was part of the perimeter wall.

Captain Reyes had joined his crew and watched Tim disappear around the side of the building.

"Hector, we have you surrounded. Give us the children." Reyes hoped to distract Hector. A shot rang over their heads in reply.

Reyes and his team held their collective breath; time stood still. Then there was a loud *crack* followed by "Oomph!"

"All clear," Tim advised. Reyes raced into the dorm and found Raoul out cold on the ground and Hector contained by Tim. "Check the children. Emma! Liam!"

Maria did a quick scan of the small group huddled against a side wall. "They're not here!"

"How can that be?" Tim shouted. Pulling Hector to his feet, he got face to face and belted out, "Where are Liam and Emma?"

"Don't know, I'm sure they went to bed with the rest of them."

Tim was not going to be put off so easily. "That girl, the young lady that was in the compound with them … where is she?"

"I keep her in lockdown." Hector chuckled. "There's a cell by the office …"

Tim didn't need to hear anymore. He remembered the door he had seen when they visited the first time. Shoving Hector at Captain Reyes, he took off. Running toward the office, he saw the cell door ajar. He barged in without warning, but none was needed. The room was empty. Then the alarm went off in his head. The second buyer, the car he saw leaving when they arrived. Had Hector double-crossed him?

He stepped out into the courtyard and saw Reyes' team lining up the small band they had overtaken. Tim headed straight for Hector.

"Who did you sell them to?" His voice reverberated like a shockwave.

"I didn't sell them … yet." Hector played with Tim's rage.

Tim punched him directly in the face then turned to Reyes. "We have to find that car."

Reyes didn't know what Tim meant but he knew that Emma and Liam were gone.

Tim squatted in the dirt yard and dropped his head in his hands. Maria touched his shoulder lightly, hoping to console him. There was no solace. Tim felt he'd failed.

He turned to Maria, frustration in his voice. "What will I tell their parents?"

CHAPTER 17

Tim spent the morning and a good part of the afternoon at the police station helping Captain Reyes handle the band they had rounded up at the orphanage. As it turned out, only Hector and his sidekick, Raoul, knew anything about the children. The rest of the gang had just been brought in for backup. Captain Reyes and Tim wondered how Hector had been alerted. Where had they slipped up? But after long bantering, they finally got out of him that a drone flying over the compound had raised his suspicion. "It was very out of place for the neighborhood," Hector had explained.

Tim was trying to put the pieces together: the car leaving the scene this morning, the second buyer, the missing girl. How did the drone fit in?

"Were they in on the kidnapping of Liam and Emma?" Tim had no patience.

"They kidnapped them from me, they promised me money … if you find them, tell them I'm coming for my money." Tim ignored Hector's cocky attitude.

"Who's the girl that was at the compound the day we were there? The one that Liam hid behind? Is she in on this?" Tim needed as much information as he could get to track down the Walker children.

"Her name is Christine. She was messing up my operation, so I was teaching her a lesson."

"What does that mean, did you kidnap her too? What's her connection to these kids?" Tim wanted to punch the guy again but restrained himself.

"As far as I know there was no connection, the kids just took a shine to her … and well … I guess she took a shine to them."

"Go on … tell me how she got them out!"

"I really am in the dark on that, but I guess I should have taken her father a bit more seriously."

"Her father? What does he have to do with Liam and Emma?" Tim's hands were shaking; he wanted to wrap them around this guy's throat.

"Nothing." Hector was done with the shakedown. "Look, I know nothing about them. Somehow, the parents found Christine. They came to the orphanage and wanted her back. I told them they'd have to pay for her. It was the least they could do to make up for jumping in on my territory … Christine said she wouldn't leave without the kids, so I upped the price. Thus, the second buyer." Hector was done. Leaning back in his chair, he crossed his arms over his chest and gave Tim a defiant look.

Tim understood that he had gotten as much information as Hector was going to provide, but he needed to know one more thing. "Do you have their phone number?"

Hector locked his steely eyes on Tim. "NO!" he spat back.

Tim stomped out of the room.

****

Leaving the police station, Tim realized he hadn't eaten since early that morning. He grabbed a bite and took it back to his hotel. He wasn't looking forward to his next task. Standing on the balcony of his room, he listened to the soothing sound of the surf rolling over the sand. It did little to calm his jagged nerves. He played over in his mind what he would tell William and Alicia about his failure to rescue their children. He had texted them about the ongoing operation and had assured them the kids would be safely in his hands today. Now the tables were turned, and he struggled for an explanation for how things could have gone so wrong. One thing for sure, he wasn't going to quit until he tracked down Christine and her parents. Hard telling where they would take the children next, but he didn't imagine it would turn out well. After all, Hector had said Christine was working his territory. She had to be up to no good.

Taking a deep breath, he walked across the room and grabbed his phone. *Time to get this over with*, he thought. He closed his eyes, waiting for the call to go through. It only rang once, and Alicia picked up.

"You have them!" It was a statement not a question. Her excitement was overwhelming.

Tim was confused. "Wait, wait … I called to tell you that Liam and Emma were *not* at the orphanage when we raided it this morning." There, he had said it!

"But I spoke with a Christine, she called and said she had them. I figured this Christine was with your team. What do you mean, are they still missing?" Alicia went from ecstasy to mourning in one sentence. She began sobbing.

"OK, tell me —" Tim was cut off by Michael.

"What happened, who is this Christine?" Tim felt the confusion in Michael's voice.

"I'm trying to put the pieces together. Apparently Christine was being held at the orphanage with your children, but her parents came to rescue her right before we hit there this morning, and for some reason they took your kids."

"She sounded really nice on the phone, she said she would get the kids to us."

"Okay, start from the top, give me the whole conversation. Did she make any threats or demands?" Tim was back in his element, gathering information.

While Michael relayed the entire conversation, Tim jotted notes.

"One final thing: Did she leave a phone number?" It didn't sound like she planned any harm to Emma and Liam, but he had to find this Christine before she disappeared with the kids.

"We were really so excited when she called … well, we thought she was working with you … ugh …" Michael's voice dropped to a soft whisper. "No."

Tim wasn't disappointed. "Did she call your phone?"

"No, she called my wife's … she said Emma knew the number. Wait …" Tim heard him digging around, then a triumphant yell. "Here, this is the number she called from." As he rattled it off, Tim jotted it down.

"Sit tight, I can track this down. We'll have your kids in safe custody tonight." As he hung up, Tim hoped that he could make that promise come true.

CHAPTER 18

Tim was with Captain Reyes and his team surrounding a modest condo complex, preparing for their second raid of the day. After he'd hung up with William and Alicia, Tim had phoned the captain. Explaining the conversation he'd had with the Walkers, he gave the phone number to Reyes. By the time he'd arrived back at the police station, Captain Reyes' team had tracked the number to their current location.

Tim used Google Earth to investigate the layout of the condo. By tracking the number, they knew exactly which unit might be harboring Emma and Liam. Devising a quick plan, the team had departed the station less than an hour after Tim's call to the Walkers.

Moving quietly in the darkness, they surrounded the condo unit and were waiting on Tim's signal to move. He had reiterated over and over, "No shots." He didn't want to take the chance that the children might be caught in the cross fire. They had agreed to pack Tasers.

Standing outside the front door, Tim knocked aggressively. Captain Reyes and Maria were sheltered from sight, one on each side of the doorway.

There was no answer.

"I know they're here," Tim whispered. He pounded harder, holding his breath, hoping this was going to go down better than the morning raid.

"Wait." He heard feet shuffling than an answer.

"Who is it?" A man's voice, an accent he didn't recognize. Tim figured it was Christine's father.

"Is Christine home?" Tim set the bait.

"She's turned in for the night," came the reply behind the door.

"It's really important, this is an emergency." Tim knew a mystery always produced a response. A few seconds of silence, then the rattle of the deadbolt. The door opened a few inches.

"Who are you, what do you need Christine for?" An eye peered through the crack.

Tim stuck with his story. "Can I speak with her for just a minute? It's life and death." Thinking of Liam and Emma, he felt that part was true. The door opened a few more inches, Tim took the advantage and stuck his foot into the doorway.

"Hey!" The man behind the door yelled in a gruff voice.

Using the full weight of his body, Tim shoved the door fully open, knocking the man off his feet. Captain Reyes and Maria followed Tim into the room, Tasers ready. The racket woke the entire house. Within minutes, two ladies emerged from separate rooms, wearing stunned expressions when they saw a police officer holding the man of the house on the ground.

Tim recognized Christine instantly and headed across the room toward her. "Where are they?" he bellowed. He didn't need an answer, because two little heads peered around the door. His heart filled with relief.

"You're under arrest for kidnapping." Captain Reyes was pulling Christine's father to his feet. Maria was headed for the other lady in the room.

Amongst all of the confusion, both children started to cry. Christine stooped down and wrapped them in her arms.

"You're Tim, correct?" Christine's dark eyes were filled with relief. "I'm so happy you're here, you can get them home."

Tim was a bit confused but could see she meant the children no harm. "Yes, but first we need to take all of you to the station to get this sorted out. We may be pressing charges against your parents."

"Oh, you will," Christine spoke assuredly. "Come with me, I'm not going to leave anyone behind again." She headed toward the door.

"Christine!" her father barked. "Don't!" Tim could feel the static charge between them.

"I'm not going to be a part of this anymore." She backed her father down with her harsh rebuttal.

"You can't do this to me, after all I've ever done for you."

"My whole life we've been moving from one moment of terror to the next, then you drag me into your operation without giving me a choice. I'm done, I want to choose my own life." Then looking at Tim, she softly added, "Follow me." Grabbing a pile of keys off the table at the front door, she exited the condo and headed across the common to another unit. Approaching the unit directly across the grounds, Tim noticed locks on the outside of the door.

Strange, he thought. As the word went through his mind, Christine spoke, "This isn't going to be pretty." She fiddled with the locks and then threw the door wide-open.

Tim stepped in as Christine hit the lights. *She was right*, he thought as he digested the scene. Spread throughout the room were eight small cots. Chained to each was a frightened, disheveled young lady.

Captain Reyes was a step behind Tim entering the room, a gasp slipping through his lips.

"Jesus, Lord Almighty," he muttered.

"Looks like we've broken up two trafficking rings in one day." Tim grasped the captain's shoulder. "It's going to be a very long evening."

****

Officer Maria took Emma and Liam home with her while Captain Reyes and Tim sorted out how all the pieces fit together. The other officers that had assisted in the raid stayed behind to handle the young women that were being held hostage. Each one would be checked out by a doctor, questioned to gather information regarding what had happened to them and then hopefully reunited with their families.

Tim sat in a small room with Christine, who sipped slowly on a strong coffee. He studied her dark eyes. She was obviously a young woman; how did she get mixed up in this? When she finally set the cup on the small table beside her, Tim decided it was time to get answers.

"What were you doing at the orphanage?" Tim spoke in a soft tone.

"That Hector guy kidnapped me." Her answer was blunt.

"He said you were invading his territory. What does that mean?" Tim needed to know how deep she was in this racket.

Christine let out a big sigh then spilled all the beans. She started with her part in capturing the girls, how she would work a bar for a few days, find a mark and then, using a knock-out drug, deliver them to her parents. She knew they were being used for sexual exploitation but swore she had nothing to do with setting them up with "Johns."

"Do you understand you are complicit in this crime? This is considered aggravated kidnapping and carries stiff penalties. You are very young. I would hate to see you spend your life in prison." Using a little scare tactic, Tim hoped to get more details on her parents' operation.

Tears escaped and rolled down her smooth taupe cheeks. There were a few minutes of silence, and Tim wondered if she was weighing her options.

Christine closed her eyes and then began to speak. "I'm as much a victim as those girls in that room. I wanted out but there was no way for me to escape either."

"How's that, were your parents threatening you?"

She opened her eyes and gave Tim a hard stare. Taking a deep breath, Christine told Tim the whole story. Starting with her youth in Kosovo during the war and her father's part in the Kosovo Liberation Army. She had very little information on his operation in Kosovo after the war but knew he'd had a harsh falling-out with his partner. That's when they'd come to the US on a refugee visa. At first, she was so happy to be in America. She'd received a scholarship, was going to college and hoped for a new life. Then her father had pulled her into his operation. Christine explained the whole set up and how they had kidnapped girls from Wellesley College in Boston. She finished by telling him how they had left all the girls tied up in a warehouse and escaped to Mexico. By this time, she was sobbing. She had no idea why her father decided to run and no idea what had happened to those poor girls.

Christine looked physically exhausted. Tim decided he needed to let her rest, but he had one last question. "What did you have to do with Liam and Emma? Why did you take them?"

"I promised to get them back to their parents. That's all. I needed to protect them. I thought you were coming to buy them and take them to someplace dangerous." She paused for a moment. "It was the least I could do to make up for my part in all of this mess."

Tim saw that she was being honest. "OK, we'll talk more about this in the morning. For now, we both need some rest." He rose to leave, but Christine grabbed his arm.

"I want to help you take them home." Her eyes were pleading with him. "I need to keep my promise."

"We'll talk more tomorrow." Looking at his watch, he corrected himself. "We'll talk later today after we all rest."

CHAPTER 19

Tim was sitting between Emma and Liam on the American Airlines flight headed to Boston. Christina was sitting two rows up on the aisle. The past few days he'd been at the police station around the clock, going over the details of the operation that Christine's parents had in place.

Captain Reyes had been in touch with Lieutenant Down at the Massachusetts State Police High-Risk Victim Unit. The lieutenant was happy to hear that the missing link to her case had been resolved. The girls they'd rescued had only little bits of information, mostly due to their drugged condition while being held captive. Lieutenant Down explained that the girls' rescue was a bit of a miracle due to the tenacity of a Shelby Wilson. Why the kidnappers had pulled out so unexpectedly was not clear, but it appeared they were just a few steps behind them.

After many phone calls back and forth, it was decided that Jetmir and Debora would be extradited to the United States, as the kidnapping and sex trafficking of the girls in Boston took precedence. Once they faced indictment in Boston and were sentenced, a similar hearing would be held in Mexico.

Captain Reyes was anxious to have justice served but he had other cases to handle. They were still unraveling how deep Hector's operations went and he was determined to investigate all of the existing orphanages surrounding Cancun to be sure there was no other suspicious behavior occurring.

He had gone to his church members and explained what was going on at St. Cecil's. The parishioners were devastated by the betrayal. The pastor had decided to make up the unintended damage by caring for the children until their parents were located and came to retrieve them. The reunions would help to lift their spirits and right the wrong.

Tim had sat in with Captain Reyes while Christine had a final conversation with her parents.

Running the scene through his mind he'd realized that Christine was as much a victim of her parents as Liam and Emma were of Hector. Jetmir had set up the whole operation in America modeled after his trafficking exploitations in Kosovo. He had glared at Christine and rebuked her for turning on him. Christine had chastised her mother for not protecting her when Jetmir had forced her into the operation. Debora had no answer for their daughter other than, "Trying to survive in this world requires harsh choices."

Tim felt Christine was salvageable and had convinced Captain Reyes to allow her to make the trip with him to take the children home. She knew she may face charges in the US but she had it on her side that she too was kidnapped and had worked to protect the children.

Reliving the past few days, Tim watched Liam and Emma as they scrolled through the shows and games on the screens attached to the seats in front of them. *Kids are so resilient*, he thought. As they settled in, he closed his eyes. It was a four-hour flight — time to catch up on some much-needed rest.

****

As the flight touched down, Tim found it difficult to contain the excitement of the children. Honestly, he shared their elation and was happy to be bringing them home. It didn't always end this way, there had been touch and go moments in Cancun.

As he walked them past the security, Emma and Liam took off when they spotted their parents. They joined in a massive family hug that Tim feared could break the tiny bones of the children, but no one was willing to let go. People passing by couldn't help but get drawn into the beauty of the moment. Tim noticed tears in the eyes of many who stopped to observe.

Finally, William broke away and headed straight for Tim and captured him in a giant bear hug.

"You will never understand how grateful we are," he whispered into Tim's ear.

"I'm so thankful that I was able to return your children to you." Now Tim had tears rolling down his cheeks. He knew there had been moments when he thought he had lost them.

Emma and Liam finally wiggled free of Alicia's grasp and dragged their mother over to where Christine was watching in silence.

"This is Christine." Liam was the first to introduce her. "She took care of us and told us fun stories and made sure we were tucked in at night and made sure we played." Liam stopped to catch his breath.

Christine saw the gratitude in Alicia's eyes. Within seconds she was swept into a group hug.

"Come on." William interrupted the celebration. "We're all going out for a welcome home dinner. Where to?" he asked the children. He didn't get the answer he expected.

"Can we just go home?" Emma pleaded.

"Yeah, and order pizza," Liam chimed in.

"For sure, pizza is on me!" William grabbed them into one more bear hug. "Tim, Christine, please join us!"

"Yes, yes!" Liam added.

"Well, for a bit," Tim agreed, "then I need to get home and give my kiddos a big kiss!"

They walked together from the airport arm in arm

EPILOGUE

Christine sat quietly in the corner of Peet's Coffee Shop, waiting for Shelby and Sydney to arrive. She wasn't sure how this meeting was going to go but she'd insisted to Tim that she had to face this herself.

When they walked in, she knew immediately from their expression how they felt. The twins embraced her as if she was a long-lost friend. They sat huddled over the table and Christine told them everything that had happened to her since she had left Boston with her parents. She ended by telling them all about Liam and Emma, how they had become an important part of her life.

After her long story ended, Shelby spoke, "We were so worried about you. We knew you were forced into the actions you took."

"That doesn't make it okay, my part, what my parents did." Christine's dark eyes filled with tears. "I'm so sorry, please forgive me."

"Forgiven," Sydney exclaimed. "What happened has headed us both down a new path. The events in your life shape who you are if you don't allow yourself to become a victim of them."

"I understand what you mean." Christine grabbed their hands. "Thank you!" Then she told them about Tim and his non-profit. She'd been put on probation but it was agreed that she could serve her parole time working with Tim's organization. The courts felt it was the perfect way for her to pay her dues.

Sydney wanted to know more about "Saving Childhood," it was a group she felt she could get behind. The conversation slowly drifted around to girl talk and before long, the small huddle looked like your average college coeds having a coffee and planning their next outing.

This feels good, thought Christine as she watched the twins, for the first time in her life she felt like she had real friends.

SOLD

FACTS ON HUMAN TRAFFICKING

Human trafficking is defined as holding or transporting people, often by use of force, fraud, or coercion, for commercial or sexual exploitation. According to some estimates, approximately 80 percent of trafficking involves sexual exploitation and 19 percent involves labor exploitation.

Although slavery is commonly thought to be a thing of the past, human traffickers generate hundreds of billions of dollars in profits by trapping millions of people in horrific situations around the world, including here in the U.S. Traffickers use violence, threats, deception, debt bondage, and other manipulative tactics to force people to engage in commercial sex or to provide labor or services against their will. Victims of trafficking can be any age and gender.

Every continent in the world has individuals who are held in bondage. In the United States, it is most prevalent in Texas, Florida, New York, and California.

Education is the number-one way to prevent human trafficking! I hope this story, although it is fiction, increased your awareness of how easily one can be pulled into such a trap. If you suspect someone is in a compromised situation, please use the following contact information:

National Human Trafficking Hotline (from the National Human Trafficking Resource Center)

- 1-888-373-7888

- Website: https://humantraffickinghotline.org/

- Available 24 hours per day, seven days a week.

Can provide assistance in more than 200 languages.

ABOUT THE AUTHOR

My love of reading began as soon as I learned to decode letters. Reading voraciously, I learned how to write. My love for children guided me into the field of education. My desire to help others brought these two passions together. How can one look around the world and not want to change what they see? I write to communicate to the next generation in a way that they will hopefully strive to make our world a better place.

Find Ginger's other publications on her Amazon page: https://www.amazon.com/Ginger-Rodeghero/e/B07KRPLYXX